P9-CED-288

Let's Play, Crabby!

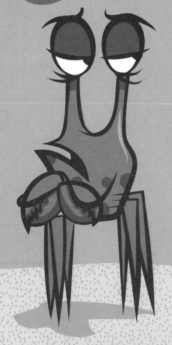

Jonathan Fenske

🌰 **ACORN**™
SCHOLASTIC INC.

For Coco, who is the best at finding things!

Copyright © 2019 by Jonathan Fenske

Library of Congress Cataloging-in-Publication Data

Names: Fenske, Jonathan, author.
Title: Let's play, Crabby! / Jonathan Fenske.
Description: First edition. | New York : Acorn/Scholastic Inc., 2019. |
Series: A Crabby book ; 2 | Summary: Crabby is a very grumpy crab, so
Plankton tries to find a game that will cheer Crabby up, but Crabby does
not want to play Simon Says or hide-and-seek—will a game of tag be more
to Crabby's taste?
Identifiers: LCCN 2018035383| ISBN 9781338281552 (pbk.)
ISBN 9781338281576 (hardcover)

Subjects: LCSH: Crabs—Juvenile fiction. | Plankton—Juvenile fiction.
Games—Juvenile fiction. | Play—Juvenile fiction. | Humorous stories. |
CYAC: Crabs—Fiction. | Plankton—Fiction. | Games—Fiction. |
Play—Fiction. | Humorous stories. | LCGFT: Humorous fiction. | Picture books.
Classification: LCC PZ7.F34843 Le 2019 | DDC (E)—dc23
LC record available at https://lccn.loc.gov/2018035383

10 9 8 7 6 5 4 3 2   19 20 21 22 23

Printed in China   62

First edition, August 2019

Edited by Katie Carella
Book design by Maria Mercado

2

SHHH!

4

7

THE GAME

I **love** to play games!

Hey, Crabby! Do you want to play a game?

No, Plankton! I do **not** want to play a game.

I do not like games.

13

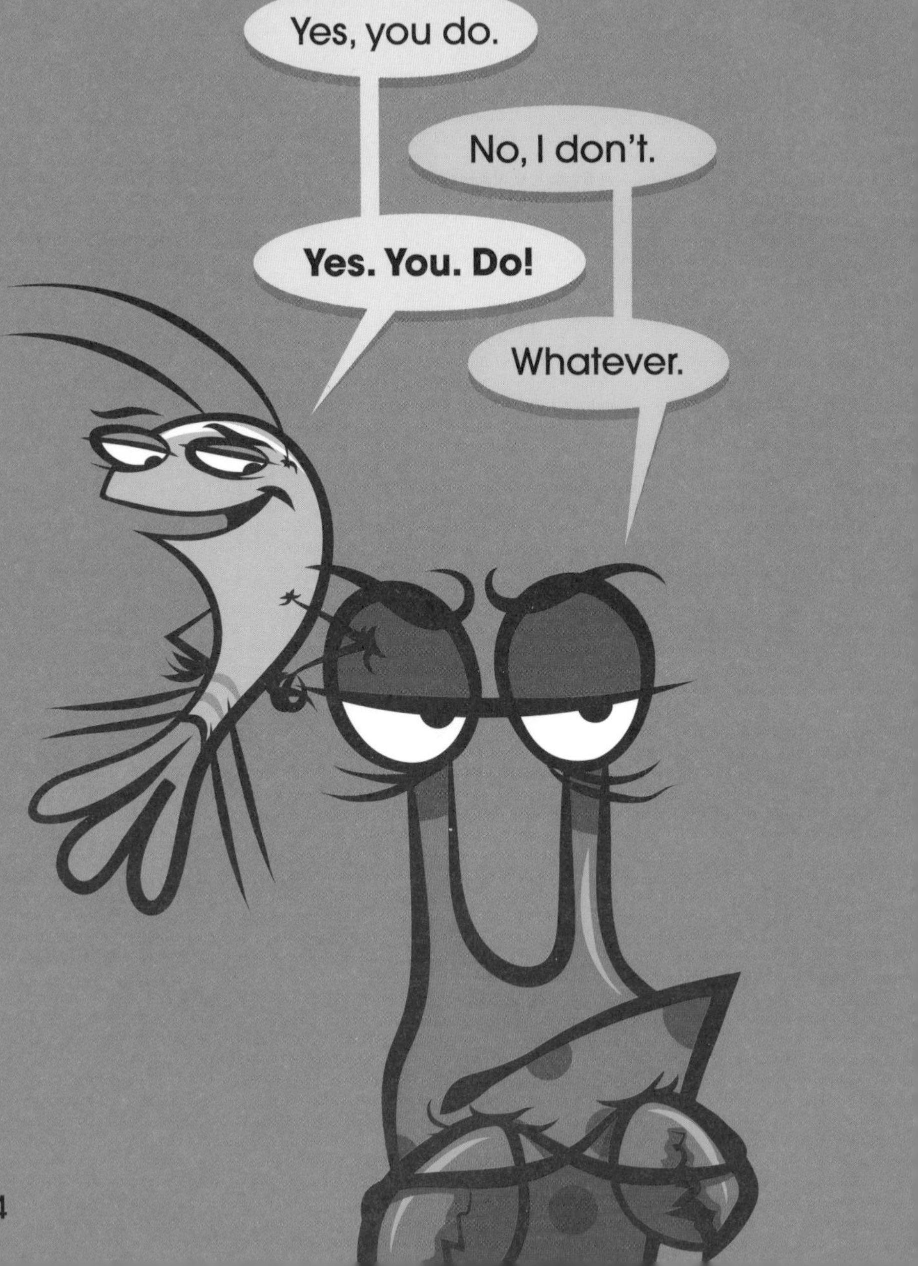
Yes, you do.
No, I don't.
Yes. You. Do!
Whatever.

15

Fine. We can play Crabby Says.

That is more like it.

17

Wait. If I say, "Crabby says," you have to do what Crabby says?

You got it!

Wow. I think I will like this game!

So, are you ready to play?

Yes!

Really ready?

Yes!

Here we go!

19

Hey, Crabby. Do you want to play hide-and-seek?

No, Plankton. I do **not** want to play hide-and-seek.

You can hide.
I will seek.

I do not **want**
to hide.

Okay. I will hide.
You can seek.

I do not **want**
to seek.

We cannot play
hide-and-seek
if you do not
hide **or** seek!

Exactly.

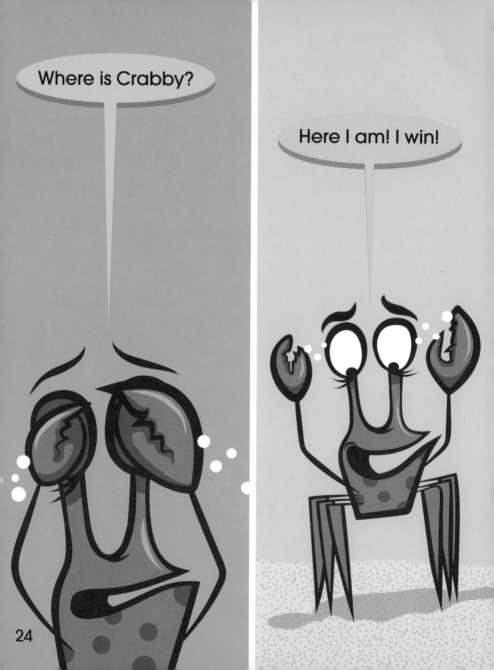

That was
no fun.

It was
fun for me.

TWITCH

TWITCH

25

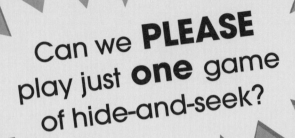

HOORAY!

Can I hide?

Let's flip a coin.

27

It is tails!

I guess **you** will have to seek.

This is **so** exciting!

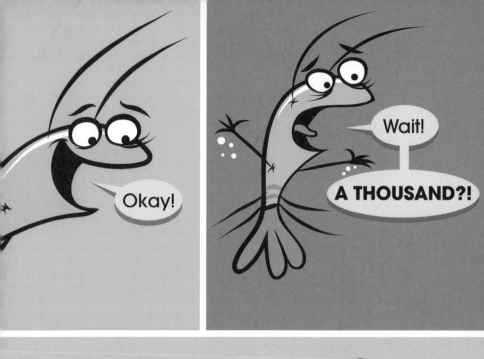

31

THE OTHER OTHER GAME

Hey, Crabby! Do you want to play tag?

No, Plankton. I do **not** want to play tag.

33

Hmmm.

Tag is **more** fun with **more** players.

Hey, Abby, Tabby, and Blabby!

You have **got** to be kidding.

Closer.

Closer.

Are you ready?

YES!!!

I cannot be IT because—

Tell me! Tell me!

About the Author

Jonathan Fenske lives in South Carolina with his family. He was born in Florida near the ocean, so he knows all about life at the beach! He **loves** to play, and playtime for him is running and climbing mountains.

Jonathan is the author and illustrator of several children's books including **Barnacle Is Bored**, **Plankton Is Pushy** (a Junior Library Guild selection), and the LEGO® picture book **I'm Fun, Too!** His early reader **A Pig, a Fox, and a Box** was a Theodor Seuss Geisel Honor Book.

THESE BOOKS ARE NOT FUNNY.

Barnacle Is BORED
Jonathan Fenske

Plankton Is PUSHY
Jonathan Fenske

YOU CAN DRAW PLANKTON!

 This is so exciting!

1. Draw half of a heart.

2. Draw the mouth and the front side of the body.

3. Add three loops at the bottom and one line across the body.

4. Fill in the mouth. Draw four legs and two antennae.

5. Add Plankton's goofy eyes and arms! Finish with a few details.

6. Color in your drawing!

WHAT'S YOUR STORY?

Plankton loves to play games.
What kind of games do **you** like to play?
Would you play games with Plankton?
Would Crabby play with you?
Write and draw your story!

scholastic.com/acorn